D0719569

This book belongs to:

_____

Contents

Ladybird

Cover illustration by Peter Brown

Published by Ladybird Books Ltd
27 Wrights Lane London W8 5TZ
A Penguin Company

2 4 6 8 10 9 7 5 3 1

© LADYBIRD BOOKS LTD MCMXCVII, MMI

LADYBIRD and the device of a Ladybird are trademarks of Ladybird Books Ltd

Printed in Italy

Time for school

written by Marie Birkinshaw
illustrated by Tony Kenyon

"Hurry up," said Mum, "or we'll be late for school."

We all rushed downstairs,
picked up our bags and went
outside. Mum closed the door.

"No, wait!" said Kate.
"I've forgotten my homework.
Mrs James will go mad if I don't
have it with me this time!"

So we all went back inside.

"Be quick, Kate," cried Mum,
"or we'll be very late for school,
and Mrs James really will be cross
with you."

Kate found her homework and rushed downstairs.

We all picked up our bags and went outside.

Mum closed the door and turned the key in the lock.

We all headed for the car.

"No, wait!" said Charlie.
"I've forgotten my sports kit
and it's football today."

So we all went back inside.

"Hurry up, Charlie!" cried
Mum. "We'll be late for school!"

Charlie got his sports kit and
rushed downstairs.
We all picked up our bags
and went outside.

Mum closed the door and turned the key in the lock. She unlocked the car and we all tried to get in the front seat.

We could tell by the look on Mum's face that this was not a good idea, so we got in the back and put on our seatbelts.

"I don't believe it!" cried
Mum. "I've forgotten my bag!
We'll never get to school
at this rate."

She took off her seatbelt and
went back in the house.

Mum found her bag and
rushed out of the front door.

She locked the door, got back into the car, put on her seatbelt and started the car up.

"Can we have the radio on,
please, Mum?" said Kate.

"OK," said Mum. "But let's get
going or we'll never get to school
today."

And the man on the radio said,

Good morning! Now for the latest news on this lovely Saturday morning...

Saturday?
I don't believe it!

WHOOPEE!

The ghost house

written by Marie Birkinshaw
illustrated by Peter Brown

This is the train
that rumbles the floor,
as it goes through the door
to the ghost house.

This is the chain
that rattles the train,
that rumbles the floor,
as it goes through the door
to the ghost house.

This is the hand
that shakes the chain,
that rattles the train,
that rumbles the floor,
as it goes through the door
to the ghost house.

This is the face
that follows the hand,
that shakes the chain,
that rattles the train,
that rumbles the floor,
as it goes through the door
to the ghost house.

This is the scream
that comes from the train
when we see the face
that follows the hand,
that shakes the chain,
that rattles the train,
that rumbles the floor,
as it goes through the door
to the ghost house.

SCREAM!

And this is the way out...

Let's go round again!

The raven and the jug

One of Aesop's fables
illustrated by Peter Massey

A big black raven wanted
a drink.

She saw a big jug with water
at the bottom. But she couldn't
reach the water.

So the raven collected some stones
and put them into the jug, one
by one.

The water rose up and up the jug
until...

At last the raven had
a long, long drink.

Moral: If you try hard enough, you can
do things that you thought would be very
difficult.

Night flight

written by Catriona Macgregor
illustrated by Andy DaVolls

In the middle of the night,
When the moon is bright
And the lightest of breezes
Are all just right,

Find a branch high up
And hold on tight.
Don't worry at all,
You'll be all right.

Just take a deep breath…
And a step to the right…
Then flap your wings
With all your might.

That's right! You've done it!
Your very first flight.

Learning to read with this book

Special features

The ghost house and other stories is ideal for early independent reading. It includes:

• a longer story to build stamina.

• two rhymes for reading fluency and memory.

Planned to help your child to develop his reading by:

• practising a variety of reading techniques such as recognising frequently used words on sight, being able to read words with similar spelling patterns (eg, night/flight), and the use of letter-sound clues.

• using rhyme to improve memory.

• including illustrations that make reading even more enjoyable.

Read with Ladybird

Read with Ladybird has been written to help you to help your child:

- to take the first steps in reading
- to improve early reading progress
- to gain confidence

Main Features

- **Several stories and rhymes in each book**

This means that there is not too much for you and your child to read in one go.

- **Rhyme and rhythm**

Read with Ladybird uses rhymes or stories with a rhythm to help your child to predict and memorise new words.

- **Gradual introduction and repetition of key words**

Read with Ladybird introduces and repeats the 100 most frequently used words in the English language.

- **Compatible with school reading schemes**

The key words that your child will learn are compatible with the word lists that are used in schools. This means that you can be confident that practising at home will support work done at school.

- **Information pullout**

Use this pullout to understand more about how you can use each story to help your child to learn to read.

But the most important feature of **Read with Ladybird** for you and your child to have fun sharing the stories rhymes with each other.